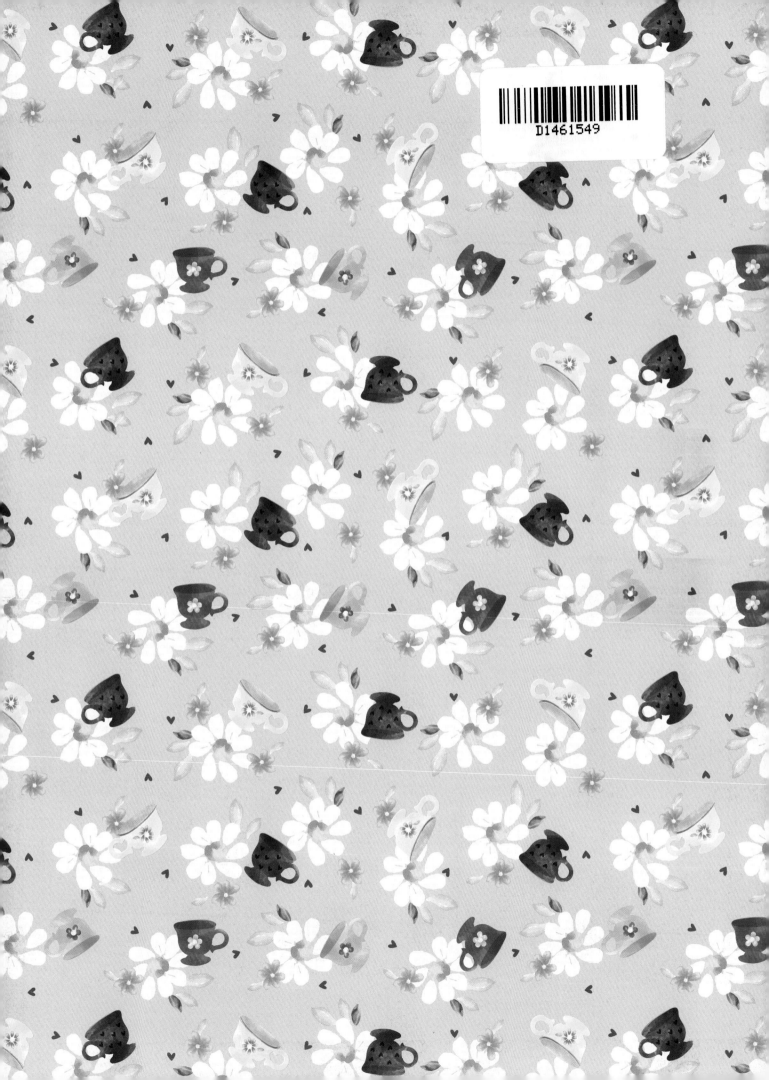

EGMONT
We bring stories to life

First published in 2015 by Egmont UK Limited,
The Yellow Building, 1 Nicholas Road, London W11 4AN
All rights reserved.

Written by Kate Graham.
Designed by Anthony Duke.

© 2015 Disney Enterprises, Inc.

ISBN 978 1 4052 7801 0
60316/1
Printed in Italy

Stay safe online. Any website addresses listed in this book
are correct at the time of going to print. However, Egmont
is not responsible for content hosted by third parties.
Please be aware that online content can be subject
to change and websites can contain content that
is unsuitable for children. We advise that all children
are supervised when using the internet.

Disney Sofia the First

Annual 2016

This special

Annual

belongs to

....

Write your name here.

Contents

Hello Sofia

Life as a Princess

Sofia's new family:
She has a stepsister called Amber and a stepbrother called James. And of course, King Roland is her new dad!

Sofia's new home:
The royal castle of Enchancia. Sofia's bedroom is HUGE!

Sofia's new school:
Royal Prep Academy, where Sofia is a princess-in-training.

Sofia's new clothes:
Sofia wears a lilac princess dress and a matching tiara. Pretty!

Sofia's new friends:
Clover the rabbit is Sofia's new best friend.

Sofia hasn't always been a princess. Not so long ago, she lived a simple life with her mother, Miranda, in the Kingdom of Enchancia. Sofia's mother worked in the village shoe shop. One day, Sofia's mother took a new pair of royal slippers to King Roland and they fell in love. King Roland and Miranda were married soon afterwards – and that made Sofia a princess! From that time on, nothing was ever the same again ...

Get out your best colouring pens for Her Royal Highness, Sofia the First!

Make a Wish!

Sofia's special amulet allows her to talk to animals. What magical power would you like? Write your wish here.

....

....

....

School's Calling!

Everybody is ready for the start of the school day. Look carefully at the colourful scene, then answer the questions.

Tick the circle next to each of these hearts when you find something the same colour in the picture.

ROYAL PREP ACADEMY

Can you spot Sofia's school bag in the picture?

Answers on page 66.

Amazing Amulet

Today we're visiting our school friend Zandar, in the Kingdom of Tangu. As soon as we get there, we jump aboard magic carpets, and we're off to Tangu Peak to have an awesome party together!

But suddenly our carpet starts behaving in a strange way, and it turns upside down. "Stop!" I cry.

Oh no! Our carpet doesn't listen to us, and flies in another direction. "Stop it!" Zandar and James shout.

Then the naughty carpet flies right into some big hanging gardens. We can't control it! "Brace yourself!" I tell Amber.

Once we land in the gardens, I try to find a way out, but the vegetation is too thick. What can we do?

Just then my amulet starts glowing! Every time it glows, magical things suddenly happen! And this time?

I can't believe my eyes! The amulet called Princess Jasmine, so that she can help us get out of here.

Amber is surprised to see Princess Jasmine, but I don't tell her about the powers of my amulet. Jasmine says that our carpet is wild, and that we have to be firm if we want it to listen to us. This might be tricky ...

Amber and I try to follow Jasmine's advice and ... the carpet lets us get aboard! Wow!

"Take us to the Tangu Peak!" I say firmly. And the carpet flies us out of the gardens. Success!

Hurray! Princess Jasmine leads us to Tangu Peak. Before she leaves, we thank her warmly, but she says that she just helped us rescue ourselves. We feel so proud as we wave goodbye!

Unfortunately, when we land on top of the Peak, we realize that the party's over. Oh no! What a shame!

"Never mind. We had a wonderful adventure and a great time together!" Amber says.

The End

Enchanted Carpets

Sofia and her friends travel to Tangu Peak on magic flying carpets. Follow the dotted lines to see who climbs aboard which carpet. The first one has been done for you.

Colour the dots next to each friend in the right colour for their carpet.

16

COLOUR MAGIC

Design your own magic carpet
by colouring a pretty pattern
on the one below.

17

... Sofia's Friends

Robin

A song bird with a beautiful voice ... Robin is also wise. She helps Sofia make the right decisions.

Clover

This big-hearted bunny is Sofia's best friend and is also leader of the woodland creatures. He loves snacking on carrots!

Whatnaught

This squirrel smiles all the time but never speaks! Secretly, he's clever as well as very cute!

Mia

Mia is very kind and sees the good in everyone. She has a bubbly personality that is hard to resist – and it certainly makes Sofia smile.

Sofia loves playing with her forest friends in the castle garden. See if you can name them all, then colour them in.

Sofia says: "Friends sweeten the day."

19

Time for Tea

Sofia is having tea in the garden with her animal friends. The pictures look the same, but can you find 8 things that are different in picture 2?

Answers on page 66.

Princess Portrait

Use the pictures to help you read this story.
Use the pictures to help you read this story.

 Clover
 Whatnaught
 picture
 carrot
 mirror

Sofia wanted to paint a of one of her friends. She asked

 if she could paint him, but he was busy eating a .

So Sofia went to look for , but she couldn't find him

anywhere. Sofia was disappointed. But then she had a good idea.

Sofia looked in a and painted herself! When 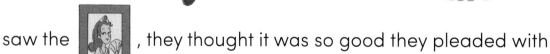 and

saw the , they thought it was so good they pleaded with

Sofia to paint a  of them. And being a kind and gracious

princess, that is exactly what she did!

 The End

Colour in the three headmistresses of Royal Prep Academy using the dots to guide you.

Flora, Fauna and Merryweather

Prancing Pairs

Sofia loves the magical flying horses of Enchancia. Can you find 3 matching pairs here?

Draw a line to connect each pair.

a

c

d

b

e

f

h

g

i

Answers on page 66.

Flying Fun

Sofia and Minimus are having a magical time flying together! Can you spot which close-up is not part of the bigger picture?

a

b

c

d

e

Magic Mistakes

Cedric has been working on a new spell, but it's gone horribly wrong! Can you spot 6 things in this scene that are out of place?

Tick a box every time you find something odd.

Secret Lesson

Hold this page up to a mirror to see what
Cedric has been practising.
Write the answer underneath.

magic

_____ _____ _____ _____

27

1

Can you put the Royal Prep Academy crests in order of size, starting with the biggest?

ⓐ   ⓑ   ⓒ   ⓓ

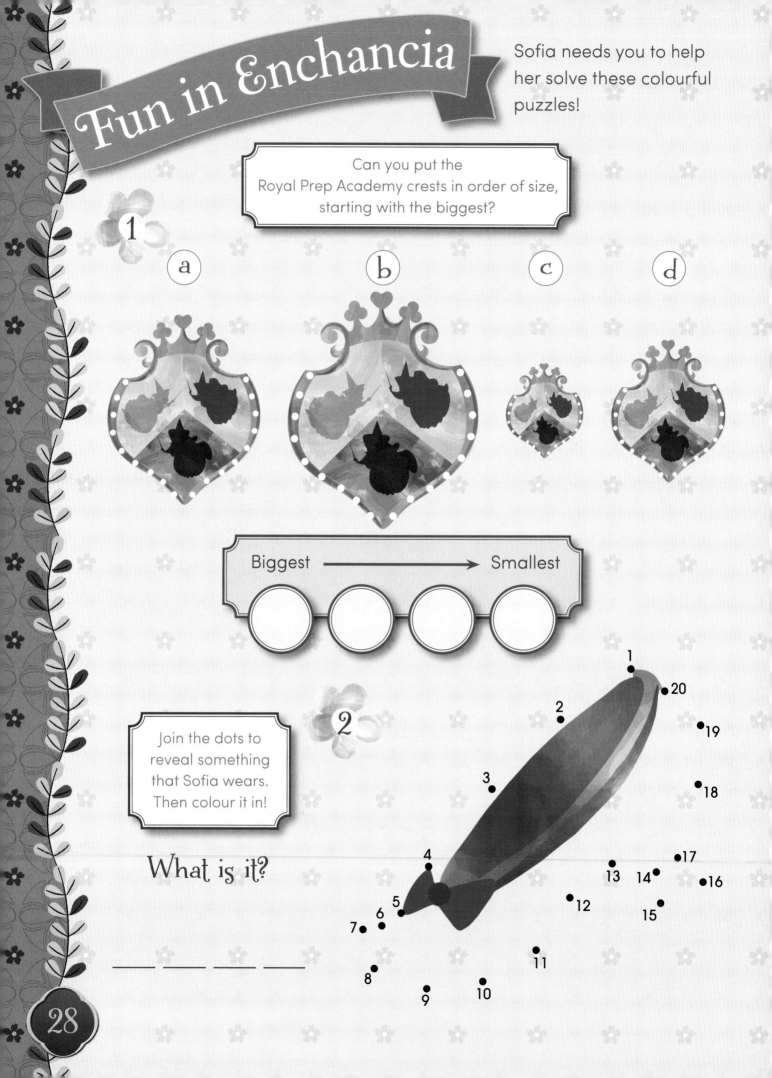

Biggest ⟶ Smallest

2

Join the dots to reveal something that Sofia wears. Then colour it in!

What is it?

___ ___ ___ ___ ___

3

There are
lots of butterflies
in the castle garden.
How many can you count?
Point to your favourite.

4

Trace over the letters
to reveal Clover's
favourite food!

carrots

Answers on page 66.

Perfect Team

Since we won the Flying Derby, Minimus and I have been training hard.
Today, we're trying a new, challenging obstacle: the hedge wall!
I'm so excited, but poor Minimus is a bit scared!

"We are nearly there!" I tell him, but he's too frightened, and he keeps slowing down. The hedge wall seems even higher …

Oh, no! Minimus and I didn't make it and he keeps slowing down as we climb. Here we are stuck on top of the hedge!

Phew! Minimus got the courage to fly down. He's sorry. "Don't worry, we'll try again!" I tell him.

But then Prince Hugo laughs at us. "You'll never make it! I wonder how you even won the Derby," he says.

"What if Prince Hugo is right? Maybe we aren't so good after all," I think out loud. Minimus suddenly goes away, and says he doesn't feel like training any more for today.

Next morning, when I pop in to the stables, Minimus tells me he won't train today either. Maybe he's a bit tired ...

I go back to Amber to ask her for advice, but Hugo comes over again and makes fun of me and Minimus. He's so annoying!

"Sofia and Minimus are the best, and they really deserved to win the Derby!" Amber shoots back. Hugo's so surprised that he can't speak!

I suddenly understand what Amber's words really mean: Minimus and I trust each other. We are an awesome team, how could I have doubted it?

I can't wait to apologise to Minimus.
Now I know why he didn't want
to train. I hurt his feelings, because
I didn't believe in him ...

... but I'll never do it again.
Minimus is the best horse
in the whole kingdom and
I love him just as he is!

WE ARE GREAT!

Now Minimus and I are ready to start
over again. I don't care how long it
will take. As a team together we can
do anything.

The End

Heading Home

After practising their flying all afternoon, Sofia and Minimus are ready to go home for tea!

1 Which trail should Sofia and Minimus take to reach the castle of Enchancia?

a

b

c

2 How many horseshoes can you count?

_____

Answers on page 66.

Princess Style

Sofia always makes sure that she dresses like a proper princess. But in one of these pictures, her outfit is a little different. Which one is it?

a

b

c

d

e

f

Answers on page 66.

Me
and
Minimus

Sharing and Smiling

Count Carefully

Get set to help Sofia count the magic things in Cedric's laboratory!

1. Find and circle 4 pictures of a potion bottle.

2. How many pictures of Wormwood the raven can you count?

3. There are 3 pictures of Cedric – true or false?

39

Who's Who?

It's the start of term at Royal Prep Academy. Can you work out where Sofia's friends went on holiday by matching the shadows to the pupils?

Draw a line to connect each child to their shadow.

LET'S TALK ABOUT HOLIDAYS

Can you find 6 school letters in the picture?

Answers on page 66.

Best Friends Album

Sofia is making a special album. She is going to stick pictures of her friends in it – Clover and the other animals, the pupils at Royal Prep Academy and Ruby and Jade. Why don't you make one, too?

You will need:

- 3 pieces of thick A3 card
- Pencil
- Hole punch
- Coloured ribbon
- Glue stick
- Sequins

Adult help needed.

Step 1

Stack your sheets of paper together as shown in the picture.

Step 2

Fold the sheets of paper in half to form your album.

Step 3

Ask an adult to help you punch four holes along the side you want to bind. You can use a pencil to mark the holes before you punch the paper.

Step 4

Pass a different ribbon through each hole from one side to another. Tie a bow to secure. Glue on sequins for a right royal cover!

TIP!
Stick a picture of yourself with a special friend in the middle of the cover.

Sofia and Clover

Make Sofia and Clover look picture perfect by colouring them in. The outlines will help you use the right colours.

How is Clover?

Sometimes Sofia is so busy that she forgets about how Clover is feeling.

Look at the pictures and colour the pink circle when Clover is looking happy and the blue one when he is sad.

a

b

c

Answers on page 66.

45

Making Friends

BEAUTIFUL!

1) Today I took a little break from the castle routine, and I've come to the village to see Ruby and Jade. Ruby shows me the lovely drawing she's just made with her new crayons.

SWISH

I'm about to make one too, when a sudden flash of blue light strikes Ruby's crayons. I've never seen anything like this before.

Oh, no! The crayons have turned into a sticky ball. Who would play such a trick? "Don't worry, Ruby," I say. "We will find out who did this."

4 "It's Lucinda!" yells Jade. Lucinda is a little witch who has just moved to the village with her family. She seems to enjoy casting spells on all the village kids.

5 I ask Lucinda why she ruined Ruby's crayons, but she runs away.

6 Ruby and Jade don't know what to do. They are very scared of Lucinda. "I'll follow her!" I say. After all, she's a little girl like us!

47

"Why do you keep casting spells on everyone?" I ask Lucinda, while she flies away on her magic broom.

Luckily, she listens to me and comes back. "No one wants to be friends with me, because I'm a witch," she says.

WHOA!

"You should try to be nice to other kids ... and I'm sure they'll like you," I say. But Lucinda thinks it's too hard for her.

"Don't worry, Ruby and Jade will forgive you, if you apologise!" I say. And off we go, riding Lucinda's magic broom!

Hurray! Lucinda apologises to my friends, and turns the sticky ball back into colourful crayons! Good job!

Lucinda says she's sorry and she promises she'll be a good witch. I'm sure we can all be friends!

WONDERFUL!

Now Lucinda knows that being nice is much more fun than casting spells on people. She celebrates our new friendship with a magic party. I'm so happy I have a new special friend!

The End

49

A Magical Party

It's party time and with a wave of her wand, Lucinda has created lots of magical decorations!

1

2

3

a

b

c

d

50

Complete this scene by matching the jigsaw pieces to the small pictures below. The first one has been done for you.

Can you spot the pumpkins?

Answers on page 66.

51

Royal Puzzles

Can you figure out the answers to these mini challenges?

1 Follow the trail and find out who Mia is flying to.

Thank you

2 Clover is giving Sofia a bunch of flowers. Hold up this message in front of a mirror to reveal what she says.

Sofia has lots of pretty things. Draw what comes next in each sequence.

3

a

b

4

a

These pictures look the same, but can you find 3 differences in picture b?

b

53

Family Time

Look carefully at this picture of Sofia and her family.

1. How many people are in the picture?

3 ☐ 4 ☐ 5 ☐

2. Who is Sofia standing next to?

Amber ☐ Queen Miranda ☐

Now cover up the picture
and answer the questions.

 3 James' jacket
is blue.

true   false

 4 Is Clover in
the picture?

yes   no

55

Answers on page 66.

Pretty Party Dress

Sofia is planning a birthday celebration for her mother. Look at the close-up pictures below to work out which dress she will wear.

Sofia will wear dress ◯

Answers on page 66.

Keep a Secret!

Find your way through the maze to discover the special place where Sofia is holding the party. Don't get lost!

Start ➡

Trace over the letters to show the name of the place where the party will take place.

Secret Garden

Answers on page 66.

Surprise Present

Sofia has a lovely birthday gift for Queen Miranda. Use the clues below to work out what it is.

(a)

(b)

CLUES

- You cannot eat it.
- It does not grow in a garden.
- It is easy to pick up.
- You use it to cool down.

(d)

(c)

Answers on page 66.

A Special Dance

Colour in this picture of happy Sofia dancing with King Roland.

A Royal Picnic

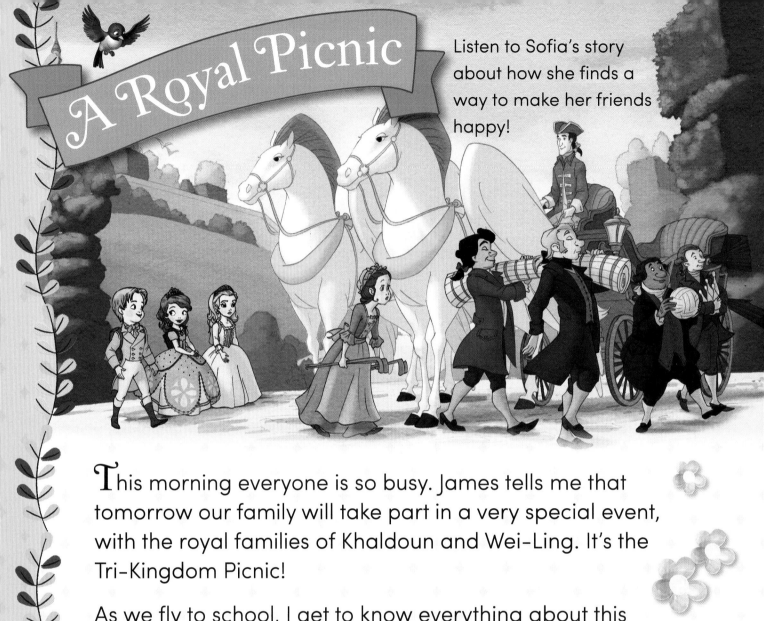

Listen to Sofia's story about how she finds a way to make her friends happy!

This morning everyone is so busy. James tells me that tomorrow our family will take part in a very special event, with the royal families of Khaldoun and Wei-Ling. It's the Tri-Kingdom Picnic!

As we fly to school, I get to know everything about this royal event. The kids will play lots of team games and it's going to be fun! But Amber doesn't look very happy.
"I'm sorry for her, but she's not very good at outdoor sports," James whispers to me.

During break-time I speak to Amber about the picnic, but she says she doesn't like sports and that maybe she won't even show up this year. Oh, no! I want Amber to be there with us!

Then I meet Maya, Jun and Leena, who are invited to the picnic, too. Maya tells me that her sister Leena doesn't like the games either. I feel sorry for Princess Leena. I must think of a way to help her and Amber.

Later, I look over at Amber during our art lesson. She loves art and decorating and always looks happy when she's doing it. I know that Leena likes spending time with Amber and learning how to be a better princess. Which gives me an idea ... Amber and Leena can decorate parasols at the royal event – I'm sure they'll love it!

Next day, I persuade Amber to come along to the Tri-Kingdom Picncic. The food is delicious and everybody is ready to play.
"Come on, Amber," I say. "There's something nice I want you to see."

I take her over to to a table covered with reels of coloured ribbons and parasols. Princess Leena is waiting there.
"Today you'll decorate parasols!" I announce.

Amber is so happy and surprised. I'm sure that she and Leena will have lots of fun. We all like doing different things, but this day will be special for all of us ...

THANK YOU, SOFIA!

The End

Perfect Parasols

Baileywick has helped Sofia gather everything Amber needs to make pretty parasols.

Just for You
Make your own princess parasol with patterns and colours you like.

Look for the items in the magnifying glasses and circle them when you find them.

Answers on page 66.

Enchancia Quiz

How much do you know about Sofia's world? Have a go at this quiz and see if you're an expert! Tick one answer for each question.

1 Flora, Fauna and Merryweather are:

- ☐ a. Sofia's aunts
- ☐ b. the castle servants
- ☐ c. headmistresses at Royal Prep Academy

2 Who does this tiara belong to:

- ☐ a. Amber
- ☐ b. Sofia
- ☐ c. Queen Miranda

3

A princess is:

a. kind and gracious

b. selfish and lazy

c. cheeky and rude

4

Cedric, the Royal Sorcerer owns a pet:

a. hamster

b. poodle

c. raven

5

Sofia is most likely to say:

a. "I can't be bothered with school."

b. "Make each day lovely with a smile!"

c. "Get me my tiara!"

Now turn to the answers on page 66 to check how well you did. Colour in the star for trying your best!

Answers

Pages 10-11: School's Calling!

1.

2. Sofia's school bag is behind the flower pot.

Pages 16-17: Enchanted Carpets

Sofia and Amber – yellow, Prince Zandar's princess friends – blue, James and Prince Zandar – purple.

Pages 20-21: Time for Tea

Page 24: Prancing Pairs

a and i, b and g, c and e.

Page 25: Flying Fun

Close-up d is not part of the big picture.

Pages 26-27: Magic Mistakes

Cedric has been practising magic.

Pages 28-29: Fun in Enchancia

1. Biggest to smallest: b, a, d, c.
2. Sofia's item is a shoe.
3. There are 8 butterflies.
4. Clover's favourite food is carrots.

Pages 34-35: Heading Home

1. Trail a.
2. There are 6 horseshoes.

Page 36: Princess Style

Picture d – Sofia's amulet is the wrong colour.

Page 39: Count Carefully!

1.

2. There are 2 pictures of Wormwood.
3. False – there are 4 pictures of Cedric.

Pages 40-41: Who's Who?

1. 1-d, 2-c, 3-b, 4-a.   2.

Page 45: How is Clover?

a. sad, b. happy, c. sad.

Pages 50-51: A Magical Party

1. 1-a, 2-d, 3-f, 4-b, 5-c, 6-e.
2. The pumpkins are on the ledge behind Lucinda.

Pages 52-53: Royal Puzzles

1. Robin.
2. Thank you
3. a-shoe. b-trinket box.
4.

Pages 54-55: Family Time

1. 5.
2. Amber.
3. false.
4. no.

Page 56: Pretty Party Dress

Sofia will wear dress b.

Page 57: Keep a Secret!

1. The party is being held in the Secret Garden.

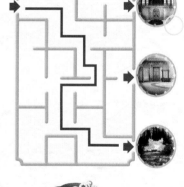

Page 58: Surprise Present

b-the fan.

Pages 62-63: Perfect Parasols

Pages 64-65: Enchancia Quiz

1-c, 2-b, 3-a, 4-c, 5-b.

Friends are Magical

PRINCESS Sofia

Have you seen our other Annuals?

Puzzles and Games

Colouring Pages

Entertaining stories

Available NOW!

disneyjunior.co.uk